This book is dedicated to all of the bunches and bunches of Celery fans. Thank you!

www.mascotbooks.com

Celery's *Greatest Race*

©2019 Bison Baseball, Inc. All Rights Reserved. No part of this publication may be reproduced, stored in a retrieval system or transmitted in any form by any means electronic, mechanical, or photocopying, recording or otherwise without the permission of the author.

All Buffalo Bisons indicia are protected trademarks or registered trademarks of Buffalo Bisons and are used under license.

For more information, please contact:
Mascot Books
620 Herndon Parkway #320
Herndon, VA 20170
info@mascotbooks.com

CPSIA Code: PRT1118A
ISBN-13: 978-1-64307-016-2

Printed in the United States

CELERY'S Greatest Race

by Amy Myhalenko

illustrated by Jason Buhagiar

Celery grew up in a small patch on Rich Products Farm. The vegetable patch was close to the farmhouse, so Celery could watch TV through the window. Baseball games were Celery's favorite thing to watch!

Celery imagined what it would feel like to run the bases. Fans cheering, heart racing. Stalks pumping towards home plate. Celery's roots were firmly planted in the dirt, but every day Celery dreamed of running.

As time passed, Celery grew bigger and greener. Soon, it would be harvest time. All of the different vegetables talked about where they would go after they were picked. Some wanted to go to stores, others wanted to go to restaurants. A few bunches hoped to go to schools to be part of school lunches. But Celery was different, and wanted to be an athlete.

The other vegetables laughed at Celery. A head of lettuce next to Celery said, "We are food! We will always be a side dish, not an athlete."

"Yeah!" a pepper said. "You can't be a runner, you're just celery."

Their mean words didn't bother Celery. Celery knew from listening to interviews with baseball players that it took determination and hard work to reach your dreams. And Celery had, well, both of those things.

Harvest day arrived. Workers carefully picked all the veggies and placed them in crates. They loaded the crates into the back of a pickup truck. Celery wiggled to the top of the crate to look out the back of the truck. Soon, the truck arrived at a market.

Celery was put on a table with other vegetables. It was a long hot day, and Celery fell asleep in the warm sun. By the time Celery woke up, the sun was starting to set and most of the other bunches of celery were gone.

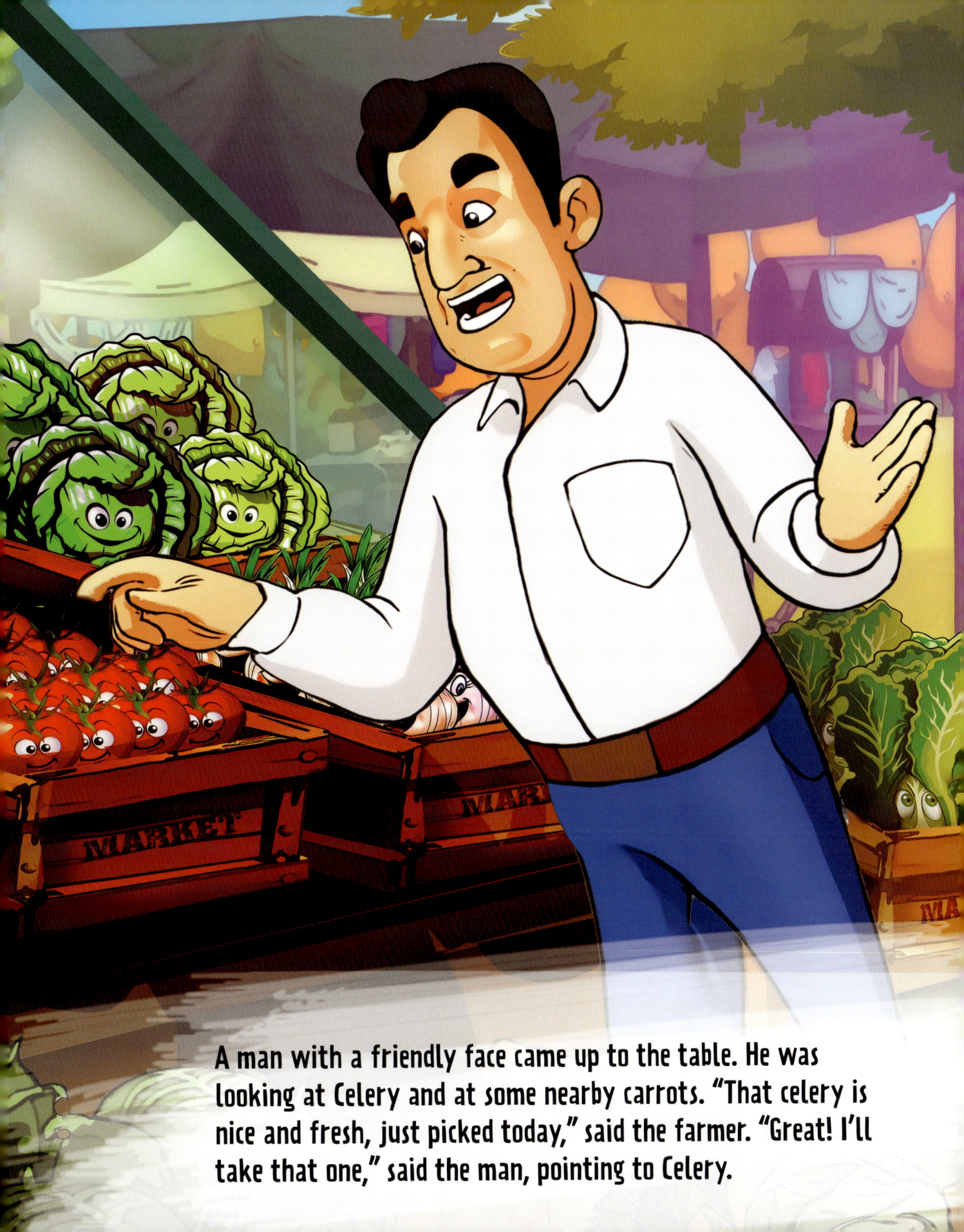

A man with a friendly face came up to the table. He was looking at Celery and at some nearby carrots. "That celery is nice and fresh, just picked today," said the farmer. "Great! I'll take that one," said the man, pointing to Celery.

The man brought Celery to a large white building. They walked through a big gate. Celery couldn't believe it. They were on a baseball diamond! Celery was so excited and started cheering. The man smiled and said, "Welcome to the home of the Buffalo Bisons."

The man brought Celery to his office. Celery looked out the window—they could see the whole field from up there! "This season we are starting a new event at the home games. It is a running race between a chicken wing, bleu cheese, and celery. I think you could be the celery we are looking for." Celery couldn't believe how incredible this opportunity sounded. "Count me in," Celery said, smiling.

The next day Celery met the other racers. Bleu Cheese was nice, but Chicken Wing was a little saucy. Celery put in lots of hours running on the treadmill and lifting weights. Celery ate healthy foods, got plenty of rest, and grew stronger every day. Training was tough, but Celery knew it would be worth it.

The day of the first race finally arrived, and the moment Celery had been waiting for its whole life was here: all of the racers stepped out onto the field. The fans cheered, and Celery was elated. Celery lost that first race, and unfortunately, the first season ended with no wins.

Chicken Wing was the season champ and bragged constantly. Celery worried about being cut from the team. "Don't worry," the boss said. "We believe in you. Just keep trying, and a win will come." Celery trained extra hard before the next baseball season.

Celery came back next season faster and stronger, but still couldn't come out on top. Despite the losses, Celery never missed a race and approached every game with a positive attitude. It was easy to stay positive because Celery always had the support of Bisons fans and felt like the main attraction instead of just a side dish.

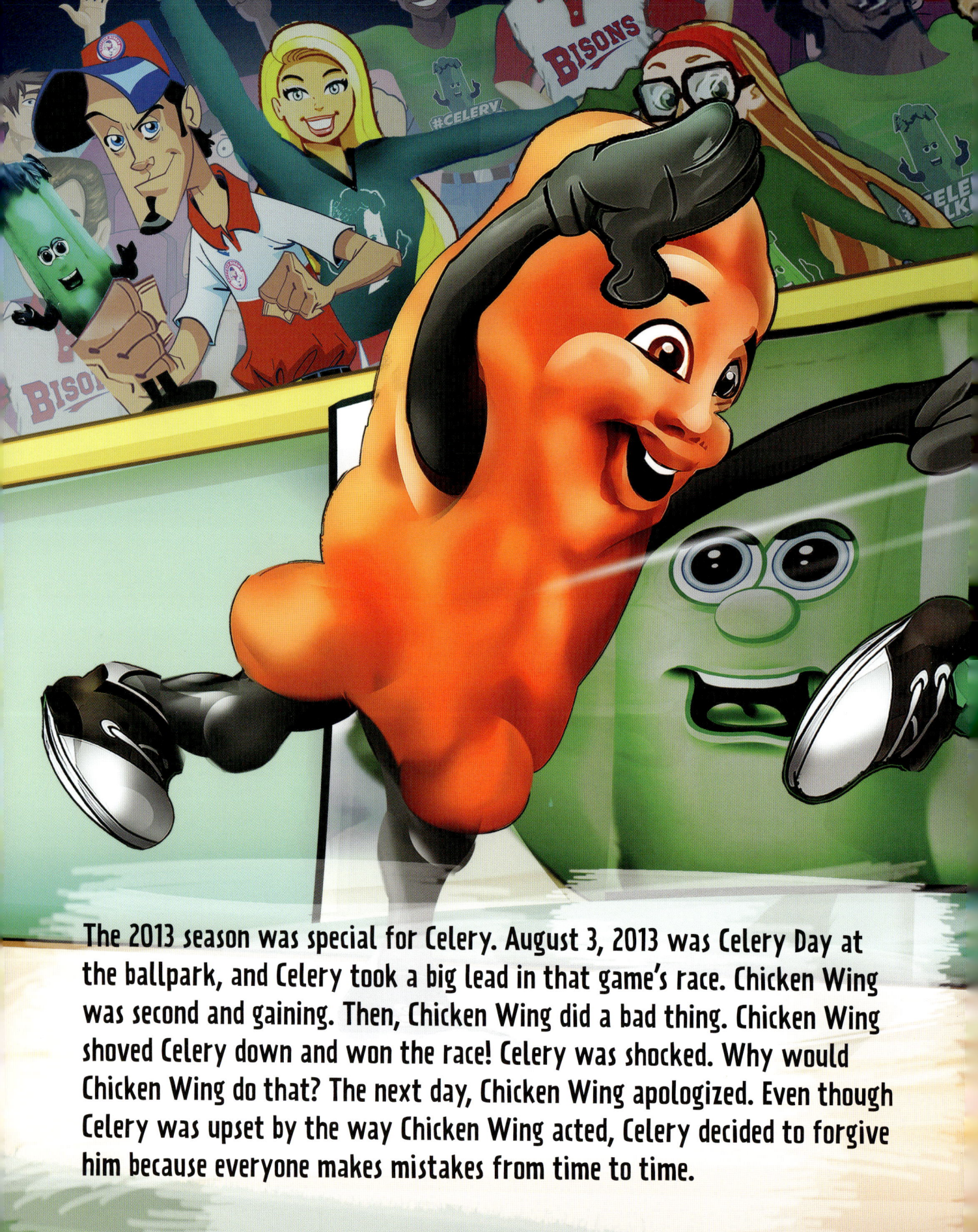

The 2013 season was special for Celery. August 3, 2013 was Celery Day at the ballpark, and Celery took a big lead in that game's race. Chicken Wing was second and gaining. Then, Chicken Wing did a bad thing. Chicken Wing shoved Celery down and won the race! Celery was shocked. Why would Chicken Wing do that? The next day, Chicken Wing apologized. Even though Celery was upset by the way Chicken Wing acted, Celery decided to forgive him because everyone makes mistakes from time to time.

Before every race, Celery looked in the mirror and whispered, "Go! Run a good race and have fun!" Celery's motto was, *If you do your best and have fun, you've already won.*

Even though each season passed without a win, Celery kept a positive attitude. All the fan support helped. It was amazing to look out and see all the celery hats and foam fingers. After one race a reporter asked Celery, "How did you find the courage to compete out there?" Celery responded with ease, "When my stalks were sore and I wanted to give up, I remembered the fans and found the strength to train a little harder."

After many years of racing, Celery made a big announcement in 2016. Celery would retire at the end of the 2017 season. The players and fans continued to cheer for Celery and hoped for just one win.

HOME OF THE BISONS

LAST RACE

On August 30, 2017 it was time for Celery's last race. After a grand introduction, the race started with Celery taking an early lead. After a brief distraction, Celery refocused and made a dash for the finish line, passing every racer in sight! Celery won! *Celery won!*

The fans went crazy! Celery finally won a race, and it felt amazing! Celery's career record was 1 – 449. But, Celery was a winner because *when you do your best and have fun, you've already won.*

About the Author

Amy Myhalenko lives in Depew, New York, with her husband, three children, and their cat. When she isn't busy selling books, she loves writing them.

Have a book idea?
Contact us at:

info@mascotbooks.com | www.mascotbooks.com